What's a Knucka?

A play

Rob Bell

BackHouse Books
California, 2022

Paperback ISBN: 979-8-9869960-0-4
E-book ISBN: 979-8-9869960-1-1

First printing edition 2022

robbell.com

Characters

Mootis Hermanicus Vulner the 12th
Thart Palls
Ornella Vapinius E. Vaponomous Montar
Reesh McTavistavish
Gary Smith
All other characters played by four chorus members

DAY ONE.

TRIPPY, BLEEPY MUSIC PLAYS as small blue and white lights begin to flicker throughout the room, celestial and pulsing. More and more colors appear as the room starts to feel like it's swirling. Lights come up revealing that the stage is the top of a mountain. We hear a fuse being lit and then… BANG!!!

A large banner drops from the ceiling with two words written on it: **DAY ONE.**

CHORUS 1 enters and walks to the front of the stage.
She speaks with a posh British accent.

CHORUS 1. *Welcome to the peak of the Banashak. The Banashak, as you can clearly see, is the tallest mountain in the region of the Fargnarthians. From the plains of Oskaro to the fjords of Prestonia, there is no taller, higher, more daunting peak than the Banashak. And no one has ever climbed to the top of the Banashak…until now.*

Four mountain climbers enter from four different directions all carrying large backpacks. They reach the middle of the stage, facing each other.

CHORUS 1. *Four climbers, from four different nations, arriving from four different directions at the exact…same…time.*

She turns and exits. The climbers stand there stunned, eyeing each other with great suspicion.

The first to speak is MOOTIS HERMANICUS VULNER THE 12TH-MOOT for short. Moot is a brute of a man, from the nation of Strovia. The word NONSTOPPER is written in large letters across the front of his jacket. He removes his wrap around sunglasses.

MOOT. *Let the record show that I, Mootis Hermanicus Vulner the 12th, was the first to solo summit the Banashak.*

To Moot's left stands REESH McTAVISTAVISH. Reesh has a

ponytail, a gold sash around his waist, and a large STONE TABLET strapped to his back. He isn't wearing a shirt.

REESH. *You are gravely mistaken my good man, for I hereby claim this singular accomplishment for the good folk of Xilna. Generations of Fargnarthians have chanted at their noon fires 'Oh great Banashak, we summon thee to thrust upon us your undulating power' while the tribes in the Zowpong River Basin have often sung 'We long for the great Mother Banashak to welcome us as a mother firkler gathers her young firklets into her arms.' And how can we forget the clansmen of the Goobachong who with their characteristic flair and flourish refer to the Banashak as 'She who cannot be mounted?' Therefore, it is with great pride that I stand before you today and proclaim that SHE HAS BEEN MOUNTED and SHE HAS BEEN MOUNTED BY ME!!! And so I dedicate this MOUNTING to my people, who have again placed their trust in me to MOUNT-*

Reesh is interrupted by THART PALLS, a tightly wound vortex of a man dressed in all black and carrying a scepter shaped like a snake.

THART PALLS. *CAP IT SCHMUCKTARD!!! Do we have to endure one more second of your speechifying? I'd rather have my eyes gouged out with a soft rubber spatula. I got here first, you got here second-actually you got here third but that level of losing doesn't warrant any mention, does it?*

He jams his scepter into the ground, folds his arms across his chest, and stares the three of them down.

ORNELLA VAPINIUS E. VOPONOMOUS MONTAR-NELLA for short-steps forward. She's wearing a purple jacket with silver trim and matching purple pants. She clears her throat and then politely speaks.

NELLA. *A bit churlish of you, to say the least, but also lacking in the esprit de corps one expects would accompany an auspicious occasion such as this. It's not so much who arrived at the top FIRST but who did it with the ease and elegance and elan of a*

*true maestro of the mountain which I believe is indisputably clear
to all present is...me.*

Moot cannot fathom what he has just heard.

MOOT. *Wait-you think you got here first?*
NELLA. *Is this not apparent to all?*
THART PALLS. *It's apparent to no one. I won. The rest of you
lost. Now I demand you exit the peak at once in an orderly
manner.*

Reesh steps forward, emphatically stomping both feet.

REESH. *Enough! You insist on this endless argufying when it is
MY footprints that are clearly etched into the soil of this summit
for all to witness-*
NELLA. *While I implore you to note MINE, which are visibly and
precisely on the ACTUAL summit, as opposed to yours, which
are off to the side.*

They each look down at their feet, and then at the feet of the
others.

NELLA. *You three may as well be standing on an altogether
different mountain.*

An exasperated grunt from Thart Palls.

THART PALLS. *But what none of you seem to understand is that
to make a claim you have to have something to make that claim
WITH. Hence my scepter, piercing the peak precisely in its center.*

He points to his scepter as if this is obvious.

Moot glances at Thart Palls' scepter and then unfurls a massive
flag-way too big to have fit in his backpack-which he drives into
the ground with great force. It is accompanied by an incongruous
loud metallic clanging.

MOOT. *But do you have a flag???!!!*

He's clearly convinced this settles the matter. He turns to Thart Palls.

MOOT. *When the plane I've hired flies overhead in two days, do you think my photographer is going to be able to see your silly little sticky stick poking up out of the dirt? Not a chance. What will be seen is the flag of the great nation of Strovia. And they will take a picture of me standing here next to this flag and that image will be beamed into every single household in my homeland...and yours as well, I might add.*
NELLA. *Not to prolong this quarrel any longer, but won't that photo have the other three of us in it as well?*

Awkward pause.

REESH. *That's a good point.*
MOOT. *I hadn't thought of that.*
THART PALLS. *Same with my plane.*
REESH. *You have a plane coming?*
THART PALLS. *And you don't?*
REESH. *I do. Two days from now. And you?*

He turns to Nella. She nods yes.

THART PALLS. *Just to double check we're all choking on the same bone here-we each have a plane coming in two days to fly overhead and take a picture of us standing alone on this peak as the first to ever solo climb the Banashak?*

Muttering and mumbling affirmations all around.
Thart Palls is a coiled mess of nerves. He begins to twitch and do an odd little jerky step.

THART PALLS. *But that's not what happened because WE ALL ARRIVED AT THE EXACT SAME TIME!!!*

His eyes bulge, he smacks his palms on his forehead.
His anguish is existential.

THART PALLS. *HOW??? HOW!!!???*

CHORUS 2 enters the stage carrying a pole. On the end of the pole is a string and on the end of the string is a stuffed bird. Chorus 2 guides the bird over the climbers heads in a series of circles as CIRCLING BIRD MUSIC plays.

They watch the bird above them.
They are transfixed.
The serenity of the moment is palpable.
Chorus 2 exits.

MOOT. *I have an idea.*
REESH. *We could use an idea right now. But perhaps you'll give us your name again?*
MOOT. *Mootis Hermanicus Vulner the 12th-Moot will do just fine. I come from the great nation of Strovia-*
NELLA. *Hence the south route.*

A look of appreciation on Moot's face.

MOOT. *Hence, the south route. Correct.*
REESH. *And your idea, Moot?*

Moot spreads his feet just a touch and crouches down ever so slightly, like he is used to being in charge.

MOOT. *We can each still win here. Because all we need is the photo, right? I just need an aerial image of me all alone on top of this mountain. That's it. So how about the three of you hide when my plane flies overhead and then a different three of us will hide when each of your planes fly overhead and ultimately we'll each get the photo we need.*

Thart Palls considers this and then audibly sighs.

THART PALLS. *And no one will ever have to know that the first ascent of the Banashak was a tie. Also known as NOT a solo climb of the Banashak.*
NELLA. *It is clever, I'll cede you that. But it contains a fatal flaw-*
THART PALLS. *And you are?*
NELLA. *Ornella Vapinius E. Vaponomous Montar. Please refer to me as Nella for that is how I am commonly known by my fellow*

Flaveyons-
REESH. *Which explains the west route.*
NELLA. *We are westerners to the bone, that is as true as the blaze of the noonday sun. My mother and her mother before that and her mother's mother's mother before that-*
THART PALLS. *Yeah, yeah-we got it...back to the flaw.*
NELLA. *The flaw?*
THART PALLS. *The flaw.*
NELLA. *What flaw?*
THART PALLS. *That flaw. His flaw. The Moot flaw. You said there's a flaw.*
NELLA. *Ahhhh yes, the flaw. We can hide while planes fly overhead. That can be done. But Moot, a logistical question for you: What is the tail number on your plane?*

Moot's shoulders slump. He did not see that coming.

MOOT. *I have no idea.*
NELLA. *So how will you know if it's your plane and not my plane? How do I know that I won't be hiding when my plane flies overhead and all of my fellow Flaveyons won't see me in all my Banashak glory...but you?*

Thart Palls gasps and sputters. This has pushed him too far. He bangs his head on his scepter. He kicks his bag. He gets down on all fours and pounds his fists on the ground. It is the temper tantrum of a three year old and it is a wonder to behold.
Reesh steps towards him and bends down.

REESH. *You've got the knobs turned up awfully high there, don't you my fellow mountain man? Can I distract you from your grief and agony by asking your name? We haven't met you yet-*
THART PALLS. *Thart Palls.*

He collects himself as he gets up off the ground, doing all he can to pretend like that didn't just happen.

THART PALLS. *Just an average citizen of Rogol-Fogol. That's all you need to know. And NO, I have no idea what the tail number of my plane is...*

Moot laughs.

MOOT. *Hold on! Did you say Rogol-Fogol?*
REESH. *Oh yes! Rogol-Fogol! I remember hearing about your country! Didn't your country have a civil war over grammar?*
MOOT. *Right! Wasn't it the dash between the two words? You had a war over a punctuation mark!!!*
THART PALLS. *Please. It's far more complex than that-*
NELLA. *I don't believe so. It was all over the news. We Flaveyons were fascinated. Rogol claimed that the dash between the two words belonged to them and then Fogol claimed the dash belonged to them and in no time they were declaring war-*
MOOT. *And the kings!*
REESH. *Yes! The kings! Your country is the one with the short kings with the odd habits-*
THART PALLS. *Can we not squander our time on needless reviews of long held mischaracterizations-*
MOOT. *We studied this in school! Was it King Shaz-*
NELLA. *King Shalaj-*
MOOT. *That's it. King Shalaj! The one who famously demanded that everyone working in the royal household have a lisp-*
REESH. *So that when he returned to his palace they would all say in unison 'Welcome home our king and MATH-TER!'*

The three of them think this is hilarious. Thart Palls does not.

THART PALLS. *Glad you all enjoyed that. Are we done with our brief foray into rumor and innuendo? Because right now on this mountain we are COSMICALLY HOSED. Moot doesn't know his tail number, I don't know mine-*

He turns to Reesh.

THART PALLS. *Do you know yours? What is your name?*

Reesh is so thrilled he asked.

REESH. *It is my honor to introduce myself. I come from a small village in the hinterlands of the beloved nation of Xilna. My given name in full is Reeshafesh Soontamgamonous Milepheshar Steve Sunata McTavistavish-*

THART PALLS. *Whoa there-you could hurt someone with that-let's go with Reesh, shall we? What we've firmly established is that we don't know whose plane is whose, correct?*
NELLA. *That is correct.*
MOOT. *And we don't know when, either. Which plane, when it's coming, tail numbers, what time of day-this is not the plan. This is not the plan.*

His invincible exterior dissolves as he begins to mumble to himself.

MOOT. *This is not the plan. This is not the plan. This is not the plan.*

They watch him for a beat, perplexed at his unraveling.

REESH. *Not to create too big a wave in the pond but we Xilnan's have a longstanding tradition for moments exactly like this-*

Nella holds up her hand.

NELLA. *Has there ever been a moment like this?*
REESH. *Excellent question. Allow me to continue and I trust your inquiry will be sufficiently satisfied. It is believed among my people that you are properly knobbed three times in your life.*
THART PALLS. *Knobbed?*
MOOT. *Properly knobbed?*
REESH. *Yes. Knobbed.*

He looks at them like everyone knows what this means. They stare at him blankly.

REESH. *Knobbed. Bobbed with a robin. Bent over the peter pole. Flummoxed. Pole axed. Cocked up like a muddle bundle bungle. Stiffed on a middler. Fargoed. Shafted. Caboosed. Squinched like a fiddled middler. Got your poo-food like a sunny GUT FAH.*

He turns to Thart Palls.

REESH. *Or as you, my easily agitated yet strangely compelling man just said, COSMICALLY HOSED.*

Thart Palls nods in apprehension.

NELLA. *You get three?*
MOOT. *It happens three times?*

Reesh is so happy they're starting to understand.

REESH. *Yes. Three. Our teachers say that three times in any one lifetime the universe pile drives you into a helpless heap of steaming nothingness absolutely unrelated to anything you did to cause it or deserve it, based on nothing you've said or done or didn't say or didn't do. Something terrible happens in your life for no reason. It just does. One hundred percent random.*

Thart Palls shakes his head in disbelief.

THART PALLS. *Where is this going?*

Reesh ignores him.

REESH. *When this happens-when you are absolutely sure without a shadow of doubt that THIS is one of THOSE three occasions of cosmic hosedness, then-and only then-there is a word you say that can only cross your lips three times in your life.*
MOOT. *And that word is...*

Reesh pulls out paper and pen and writes something down. They watch him intently. He holds up the paper. They gather around him and read what he's written.

THART PALLS. *Dupong?*
REESH. *Yes...but no. You are not saying it correctly. You must stress the N and the G-giving it more pathos, more weight. It wells up from deep within you, from the interior of your splangchnon, the place in which you bear the primordial drive for vitality. You undergo the word as it undulates through your bowels.*
THART PALLS. *Duuuuuuupppponnngggg...?*
REESH. *Better. But now if you were a Xilnan, you'd have already used up two of your uses-*
NELLA. *I am loath to interrupt what is so obviously a solemn*

occasion for you but you are now going to say a word? That's what you are going to do? And we are going to watch you say this word?
REESH. *Yes, precisely. And of course I would be honored if you'd join in the spirit of the occasion, merging together in harmonic union at the appropriate frequency and vibration.*

Thart Palls looks directly at the audience with his eyebrows raised like he cannot believe the insanity that is unfolding before our eyes.

Moot, meanwhile, is fixated on the point of all this.

MOOT. *And what's that going to do?*
REESH. *Going to do?*
MOOT. *Yes, exactly. What is it going to do? What will it accomplish? What will it produce? Practically speaking...*
REESH. *I am afraid I don't understand the question. I will say it, and then it will be said.*
MOOT. *Yes, but why? What does it mean?*
REESH. *I don't know.*
MOOT. *You don't know?*
REESH. *I do not.*

Thart Palls is suddenly very involved and very energized.

THART PALLS. *Wait. Wait. Wait. Your people have an ancient custom in which there's a word that you say when everything is falling apart-and you only get to say it three times in your life and you have to guess in a particular moment if THAT moment is one of those three times and people actually do this and no one knows what the word actually means?*
REESH. *Well, yes. Exactly. When you put it like that. I've never actually thought about it that way. I don't know if anybody knows what it means.*

Nella begins to walk in among them.

NELLA. *Far be it for me to speculate on another man's traditions, but it appears to me that this word DUPONG functions at the psycho-spiritual level much like a release valve for the soul. In the*

*due course of time a person accumulates an amalgamation of
pain and loss and wounds and pent-up anger and despair-no one
escapes the bumps and bruises of life, do they? But here, in this
particular tradition, is an enacted ritual in which you stop, you
pause, you still yourself in the depths of your being and you
solemnly acknowledge the gravity of the anguish in all its density
and dimension. You allow those dissonant chords of suffering to
find their proper resonance. And in doing so it loses its
confoundingly paralyzing power over you.*

The other three are in awe.
She smiles like she does this all the time.
Massage music begins to play, the kind that's played in stores
that sell crystals and essential oils.
Reesh spreads out his arms and then brings them together in
front of his chest.

REESH. *Dupong...*

He gradually begins to beam.
It is oddly moving.
He turns to the three of them and nods contentedly.
Thart Palls has no idea what to do with this.

THART PALLS. *What a burgered ass on a burnt bun this day
turned into. I don't know about you all, but I'm whipped. And I'm
not going anywhere. So unless anyone has any good ideas, I'm
setting up camp.*
MOOT. *That's a good idea.*

Chorus 2 enters holding another pole. This one has a large yellow
ball on the end of the string. The Sun. He passes it over the tops
of their heads. A few hours have passed.

MOOT. *Anybody hungry? I've got some extra power bars.*
NELLA. *How unexpectedly generous of you. I'd love one.*

He tosses one her way.

NELLA. *What??? Your face is on the wrapper!!!*

She reads the packaging.

NELLA. *'The NONSTOPPER. The preferred energy bar of Moot Vulner, adventurer extraordinaire.' OH! And here's a quote from you 'The only bar that fills me up on this nonstop adventure I call life.'*
REESH. *Profound. I'll take one.*

Moot hands him one. They both take a bite.

NELLA. *It's quite good. Tasty, even. And it says here it comes in three delicious 'Moot-approved' flavors.*
MOOT. *I've got all three right here.*

He tosses them each a few more.
Thart Palls watches all this unfold.

THART PALLS. *I can't help but notice you're giving away what appears to be a significant amount of your food supply.*
MOOT. *Just being generous with my fellow climbers.*
THART PALLS. *Well that's intriguing…because you don't appear to be having one yourself.*

Moot exhales, stares at the ground.

MOOT. *Yeah, you got me. There's a bit more to it.*
REESH. *A bit more?*

They all lean in.

MOOT. *Well…yes…but it's a little embarrassing.*
THART PALLS. *We're on top of a mountain in the middle of nowhere. No one is around for miles and miles. We're only here for a hot minute, and then we're never going to see each other again. So let it out man, let it go, get it off your chest.*
NELLA. *Yes, do tell.*
MOOT. *All right. But mind you–I didn't notice anything at first. At first it was just so exciting…*

LIGHTS DOWN ON THE MOUNTAIN. Lights up on HAMOOB ALDERVIN, the president of Nonstopper Power Bars. He's wearing a suit and standing behind a podium on the left side of the stage.

HAMOOB. *This is a huge day for us here at Nonstopper. For a while now we've sensed it was time to take our mission as a company to the next level. But we knew we needed a partner, a spokesperson, someone who embodies everything we're about here at Nonstopper. Someone…WHO LIVES IT. And you know who we thought of…because who better serves as a living symbol of what it means to be a Strovian-living a life of exploration and adventure-than Moot Vulner? So today, we're pleased to announce the Moot Power Trio Series in three delicious flavors. Who can compete with the Moot Nonstoppers? Or maybe I should ask: Who would ever try to compete without them?*

Moot steps next to him in a sport coat. He smiles stiffly.
A REPORTER appears.

REPORTER. *Moot, how does it feel to have just signed the largest sponsorship contract in the history of energy bars?*

Moot leans awkwardly over the podium.

MOOT. *Feels like we're just getting started. I'm so fired up! From here on out nothing but Nonstop adventure!*

Moot takes off the sport coat and tosses it behind him as he walks back over to the others, putting his NONSTOPPER jacket back on as he continues talking.

LIGHTS UP on the peak.

MOOT. *At first just the idea that I could see my face on the wrapper and then tear it open and enjoy...man, I can't tell you how huge that was. But then I noticed something...*

The others listen intently. He hesitates. They look at each other, wondering if they missed something.

THART PALLS. *You noticed something?*

MOOT. *Yeah…whew…this is tough to talk about…it was…I just…at first…I noticed I wasn't getting a lot of movement.*
REESH. *Movement? The bars weren't selling?*
MOOT. *No, not like that.*
NELLA. *Movement? They didn't give you extra energy?*
MOOT. *Nah-not that…*

He looks at them like he's already told them too much.

MOOT. *The toilet. I noticed that I was using the toilet…less.*
THART PALLS. *How less?*
MOOT. *It took a while for me to realize what was happening. Or to be more accurate, what WASN'T happening. One day I thought to myself 'I haven't sat on the toilet in a while.'*

Thart Palls is trying so hard not to laugh.

THART PALLS. *Do your power bars make you constipated?*
REESH. *The Nonstopper stops you up???*
NELLA. *The poetry of it alone.*
MOOT. *The pain of it alone.*
THART PALLS. *How many days?*
MOOT. *Days?*
THART PALLS. *Yes, how many days has it been?*
MOOT. *Since a proper squat?*
THART PALLS. *Since a proper squat, yes.*
MOOT. *Oh man, let me think…three, four, seven…*
NELLA. *More than a week?*
MOOT. *I shat you not.*
THART PALLS. *More like YOU SHAT NOT.*

The three of them think this is hilarious. Moot blushes.

Chorus 2 brings out the Sun again. He passes it over their heads. A few hours more have passed.

Nella pulls a large object out of her pack.

MOOT. *What is that?*
NELLA. *A table, obviously.*
MOOT. *You carried a table up here?*

NELLA. *Yes, of course. You didn't think that I wouldn't, did you?*
MOOT. *I didn't think you wouldn't, did I? I have no idea what to do with that sentence-*
THART PALLS. *Then let me clarify. It was half a nadger in a shoddy spatchcock just to get all the way up here, and you did it carrying that?*
NELLA. *I did.*
THART PALLS. *Am I going to regret asking why?*
NELLA. *To feast, naturally. Anyone can climb a mountain.*
MOOT. *Not this mountain, technically. At least not until today.*

Nella proceeds to set up the table, a chair, spread a tablecloth, and then add a candle and place setting.
The others are spellbound.
She notices them watching and pauses.

NELLA. *You must understand that for a true Flaveyon, it's about so much more than just 'getting up the mountain.' There's the WHAT, but then there's the HOW. We love the how-the style, the steeze, the flourish, the panache-HOW you do it. So when I climb, I don't just climb, I remind us all that WHATS always come with HOWS. As I have been known to say 'Climbing is like reciting a poem to the mountain.'*
THART PALLS. *I think I just threw up in my mouth. I am so thoroughly flummoxed, help me understand. Your plan was for your plane to fly over the peak and not just get a picture of you on top of the mountain, but you on top of the mountain with a table?*
NELLA. *Again, you seem to have missed the most basic essence of my intentions. Not just WITH a table, but sitting at said table, eating a meal-*

She begins unloading all kinds of food from her bag-fresh fruit and loaves of bread and tomatoes in all shapes and sizes and a wheel of cheese and several bowls of pasta. It's like clowns getting out of a car at the circus, the food just keeps coming.

NELLA. *And not just any meal, a feast.*

Moot is equal parts overwhelmed and intrigued.

MOOT. *The attention to detail alone is astonishing. Let alone the planning, the execution-I'm speechless-*
THART PALLS. *You're speechless about that? How about our shirtless comrade here?*

He points to Reesh.

THART PALLS. *Reesh here has been bare-chested with a stone tablet strapped to his back the entire time we've been up here and none of you have said a thing about it!*

Nella walks over to Reesh. She touches his arm, realizing that he's not actually bare-chested...

LIGHTS DOWN on the mountain.
SINGLE LIGHT UP on REEVO, a tailor who stands behind a large table strewn with shears, spools of thread and rolls of fabric. Reevo wears a tie and waistcoat. His sleeves are rolled up, glasses hang from his neck, and he has a tape measure over his shoulders.

REEVO. *The son hath returned!!!*

Reesh steps up to Reevo and embraces him.

REESH. *Yes I have! My man Reevo, the legend lives.*
REEVO. *You, my good man, are the legend. I've been expecting you. Word on the street is you're going for the Banashak.*

He whistles, a mix of fear and admiration.

REEVO. *That is serious. Historic. Terrifying...*
REESH. *She is another level. Which is why I'm here-*
REEVO. *I am honored you have, once again, chosen Reevo and Sons to clothe you for your next adventure.*
REESH. *You may regret saying that, because I need you to do some of this on the down low.*

Reesh sits down on the table. He lowers his voice.

REESH. *I'm older than I was the last time.*

REEVO. *Quite a bit as I recall…what's it been-six years since your last expedition?*
REESH. *More like seven. Or eight. I'm older. And things don't work as well as they used to.*

He realizes how vague that sounds.

REESH. *Heat. Body heat. I get colder faster than I used to.*
REEVO. *AHHHHH, I see. The great Reesh McTavistavish is becoming human like the rest of us. You have always climbed bare-chested.*
REESH. *It's the brand.*
REEVO. *But the Banashak? Bare-chested? That's a problem.*
REESH. *I knew you'd get it.*
REEVO. *You want me to come up with something to keep you warm that at the same time makes it look like you're not wearing a shirt?*
REESH. *You got it. And here's the thing: it only has to work from a distance.*
REEVO. *I don't follow.*
REESH. *All that matters is the photo. That's how the world works now. I just need a photo of me on top of the mountain. As long as it looks like I'm bare-chested from the plane overhead, I'm good.*
REEVO. *Got it. A shirt that looks like no shirt. And the legend of Reesh McTavistavish remains perfectly intact.*

Reevo turns and hollers to someone off stage.

REEVO. *Francine!!! Will you grab me every roll we have of brown, mud, tan, beige, flesh, naked, nude, nothing, espresso, earth, dirt, soil, raw waste, fudge Latin, farmland fusion, sand surprise, and butt cheek?*
REESH. *Easy Reevo, I need it on the down low.*
REEVO. *Of course. Your secret is safe with me.*
REESH. *And Francine, apparently.*
REEVO. *And Francine, naturally. Now, the most important question: Would you like extra muscles?*

LIGHTS DOWN on Reevo.
SINGLE LIGHT on Thart Palls.

THART PALLS. *Why do you have a stone tablet on your back?*

LIGHTS BACK UP on the peak.

Reesh is back in place.

REESH. *It's my tombstone.*

He turns his head to look over his shoulder.

REESH. *As you can see it has my name and my date of birth and then a dash-but the date of my death has been left blank. Powerful, isn't it?*

None of them respond.

REESH. *The date of my death has been left blank.*

They just stare.

REESH. *Because I don't know when that day is going to be...*

He gets no response.

REESH. *There's the dash. It's right to the right of my date of birth. But then there's nothing to the right of the dash.*

No one is getting it.
Reesh turns and directly faces the audience.
He turns back to the others.

REESH. *Don't you get it? The dash is our lives!!! The dash is what we do with our time between being born and dying. I'm inspiring people to do something magnificent and meaningful with their dash! What will you do with your dash? Can you imagine the power of a photograph of me on top of this mountain with a tombstone on my back and all of my fellow Xilnas contemplating their own dashes-what a potent reminder to inhale deeply of one's life!*

His explanation does not have the effect he thought it would.

They gather around the tombstone and squint and stare.

THART PALLS. *Uhhhhhh…I hate to break it to you but your tombstone here is blank.*
REESH. *Finally, you're grasping the significance! Yes, it's blank! What will you do with your dash? Now do you get it?*
THART PALLS. *Yeah, yeah, we got that a while ago. It's just that the entire tombstone is blank.*
NELLA. *There's nothing written on it.*
REESH. *Oh you are an amusing crew, aren't you?*
MOOT. *No, they're serious. This thing is blank.*

Reesh begins to tremble, and then mumble while his fists clench.

REESH. *Orpul! Bromhules! Stifmiffler! Conchica Contrapen-sensar…*
NELLA. *Calm down, take a breath, get a hold of yourself-what are you saying?*
REESH. *My brother!*
NELLA. *Your brother?*
REESH. *That's my brother. Orpul Bromhules Stiff-we call him O. And his only job was to prepare the tombstone. All the planning, all the training, the relentless attention to detail, and all he had to do was this one task. And in this he has failed me.*
MOOT. *Or…you could take off the tombstone.*
REESH. *Take it off now? I cannot endure the shame.*
MOOT. *No, no, you're good. Trust me here.*

Moot grabs the tablet, Nella pulls on the straps, Thart Palls reluctantly joins them and pulls the straps on the other side. Moot turns the tablet around and sets it in front of Reesh.

MOOT. *It's all right here.*

The other side has exactly the inscription that Reesh spoke of. He is jubilant.

REESH. *Yes! Yes it is! Sir Mootis you are a wizard-like man of great magic! How did you perform such a wondrous work in just a few seconds???*

THART PALLS. *Relax there Reesh, your brother put the tablet on backwards.*
REESH. *But how did Moot inscribe it so quickly?*
THART PALLS. *He didn't, he simply turned it around-*
REESH. *But I don't see any tools in Moot's hands-*

Reesh is so lost.

REESH. *Well…let's not get hung up on the details, let's just enjoy the miracles when they appear, shall we?*

LIGHTS DOWN on the peak.
SINGLE LIGHT on WILVIS VULNER, who stands next to his teacher's desk holding 3x5 cards. Behind the desk sits his teacher HELENE WEEBNERS. She nods at him to begin.

WILVIS. *This is my Uncle Moot. He's more famous than your uncle. Or your dad. He's a living legend. He climbs up mountains. And then he climbs down them. And then he picks a different mountain and he climbs up that one. And then he climbs down that one. I'm so happy he came to our class for career day. Does anybody have a question for my uncle?*

Moot stands next to Wilvis.
Helene calls on a student named JOONEE. Her voice comes from behind the audience.

JOONEE. *How is climbing things a job? My friend Keelza and me climb things all the time and we never get paid for it.*
MOOT. *Well Joonee, how about you tell me what kinds of things you climb?*
JOONEE. *Piles of stuff. The roof of Keelza's garage. There's a tree in the ravine by my house. We climbed that once. At night. IN THE DARK. Once, we climbed up on the roof of my dad's truck.*

Moot scans the class.

MOOT. *Can any of you do what Joonee and her friend do?*

Moot pauses a beat.

MOOT. *Joonee, look around the room. Every hand is raised. That's why you don't get paid for it, anybody can do it. Listen, Joonee, it's very important for you to understand: you just aren't that special.*

Helene calls on another student.

HELENE. *Yes, Gretchiss.*
GRETCHISS. *Do you have a girlfriend?*
HELENE. *Gretchiss!!! That isn't the kind of question we ask our guests. It's career day, we ask questions about careers-*
MOOT. *No. I don't have a girlfriend. Why would I do that? You have to eliminate everything that's between you and greatness. If you want to do something awesome you have to focus and that means you have to get rid of all the distractions in your life.*
HELENE. *Love is a distraction for you, Mr. Vulner?*

The chemistry is obvious.

MOOT. *Uh…well…I don't mean to say that you can't…I probably said that wrong. What I meant to say is that you have to be disciplined.*
HELENE. *So that's the key to life? You have to be disciplined? You say no to all those ridiculous stirrings in your heart and silly desires in your soul and then you just scamper up a mountain and it all magically works out?*

Moot is very flustered.

MOOT. *No, no, I'm just trying to help the kids here see that you have to make plans. And then you work hard. And then you just do it. And you can't ever give up.*
HELENE. *Are there any other clichés you can think of while you're at it?*

LIGHT DOWN on the classroom.
Chorus 2 appears with the MOON on the end of his pole. Dusk.

LIGHTS UP on the peak.
Each climber now has a tent in their spot.
Thart Palls pulls his scepter out of the ground.

THART PALLS. *Well, my fellow climbers destined for an infinite loop of devastating shame and failure, I would love to extend this revelry deep into the night but I've been bludgeoned by the ice cold hammer of humiliation enough for one day. I'll see you in the morning. Unless, of course, any of you leave during the night.*
MOOT. *Not me.*
NELLA. *Or me.*
REESH. *It appears we are all here to the end.*

Each sits in front of their tent.

LIGHTS DIM on the peak.
SINGLE LIGHT on Thart Palls. He's twisting off the top of his scepter.

SOLONIUS MANIFORD appears next to his tent.

SOLONIUS. *King Shalaj demands your prethence in the throne room at one-th.*

Thart Palls rolls his eyes. He follows Solonius across the stage.

SINGLE LIGHT on KING SHALAJ, sitting on a large throne.

KING SHALAJ. *The sons of kings do not climb rocks!!! Boys climb rocks. Children climb rocks. Civilians climb rocks. Royalty do not climb rocks!!!*
THART PALLS. *It's called mountaineering-*
KING SHALAJ. *Mountaineering???!!! We do not 'EER' mountains. We name mountains. We rule mountains. We own mountains.*
THART PALLS. *And soon we will be able to say that we climb mountains. Mountains no one has ever climbed. Thanks to your very own son.*
KING SHALAJ. *My son will stay and take his rightful place in doing what we have done for generations. We run things. We build things. We accomplish actual things in the actual world. We do not run from our responsibilities, we embrace them.*
THART PALLS. *AHHHHHH!!! Do you know what we are known for in the world?*
KING SHALAJ. *I do. Strength and determination and the fierce will to prevail regardless of the obstacles placed before us!*

THART PALLS. *No dad, we're not. We fight over punctuation marks. We rig every setting to make us appear to be more than we actually are. And the lisps, dad, the lisps! Everywhere I go that's all people want to talk about.*
KING SHALAJ. *Then maybe you should go less places. And stay home more.*
THART PALLS. *That's your response? Stay home more? Why? So I can only be surrounded by people who have never left?*
KING SHALAJ. *How long will you subject me to this drivel?*
THART PALLS. *It's the truth. Don't you get it? I'm not climbing for me, I'm climbing for us. I'm climbing for the future. I'm climbing for you!!!*
KING SHALAJ. *How long must I endure this onslaught of verbal diarrhea? You listen to me: I'm going to let you fumble your way up this little hill of yours. And if you make it home, having accomplished your feat, I will then watch to see if this has any effect whatsoever on our role and reputation in the world. If it does, I will be the first to concede that I misjudged the nature of your escapade. But if you fail-if I do not see a photograph of you standing all alone on top of that mountain-then when you return to the great nation of Rogol-Fogol it will be as an average, ordinary citizen because you will not be returning as my son.*

LIGHT DOWN on the king. Thart Palls goes back to his tent, where he unscrews the top of his scepter and pulls out a sword. It is long, and sharp.

Ominous music plays as he slowly begins to sharpen the sword, glancing at the tents of the others.
You could end someone's life with this sword.
You could end three lives.

SINGLE LIGHT up on Moot, who checks to see if anyone is looking before he pulls a gun out of his bag and holds it up to check the sight.

LIGHT DOWN on Moot, up on a NEWS ANCHOR, sitting behind a desk.

ANCHOR. *Welcome to the evening edition of Strovia Now. The bodies of five mountain climbers were found early this morning* *deep in a crevasse on the western side of Mount Dinvy. Details are only now beginning to reach us of an expedition gone horribly wrong. Initial reports indicate that an anchor clip wasn't properly secured and double checked. Five lives lost because of one, simple, careless mistake.*

Anchor pauses, she's listening to her producer in her ear.

ANCHOR. *We've just learned that a sixth climber has survived and is in critical condition. His name…is Mootis Vulner.*

LIGHT DOWN on anchor.
LIGHT UP on two LAWYERS, sitting at a conference table across from Moot.

LAWYER 1. *And then what did you do?*
MOOT. *Checked the tension on the rope.*
LAWYER 2. *Why?*
MOOT. *Because that's protocol.*
LAWYER 1. *And then what?*
MOOT. *I secured the clips.*
LAWYER 2. *Which clips?*
MOOT. *The clips.*
LAWYER 1. *How many?*
MOOT. *However many there were.*
LAWYER 2. *And then what?*
MOOT. *I checked the ropes, again.*
LAWYER 1. *What ropes?*
MOOT. *THE ropes.*
LAWYER 2. *And then what?*
MOOT. *I repeated the process with the ropes for the others.*
LAWYER 1. *What ropes?*
MOOT. *The same ropes I just told you about.*
LAWYER 2. *Those ropes?*
MOOT. *Those ropes.*
LAWYER 1. *Anything else you'd like to tell us?*
MOOT. *No.*
LAWYER 2. *Anything you've left out that you want included in the official record?*
MOOT. *No.*
LAWYER 1. *Let me remind you that all of this is being recorded*

for the official account.

Lawyer 1 gestures to the recording device on the table.

MOOT. *I'm aware of that.*
LAWYER 2. *In Article 4 Phase 9 Form 7 it states quite clearly that fasteners are always double checked FIRST, BEFORE the clips are secured.*
MOOT. *I know that.*
LAWYER 2. *Your testimony seems to indicate that you don't.*
MOOT. *I can only imagine how it appears to you sitting in dry clothes in a heated room indoors with a full meal in your stomach. But when you're on the mountain and a storm is coming and night is falling and the wind is tearing through your clothes all the way down to your bones and you can't hear what people are saying because the gusts are so loud and your hands keep locking up because you can't move your fingers and you're hungry and tired and scared and you're just trying to stay alive-*
LAWYER 2. *We're not interested in variables, Mr. Vulner. We're interested in process. Order. Code. Protocol. What happened and then what happened next.*
MOOT. *Someone died. That's what happened. And then someone else died. That's what happened next. And then someone else died.*

Moot grabs the recorder and speaks into it.

MOOT. *It was an accident. Got that? Got that for the official record?*

LIGHT DOWN on the lawyers.
LIGHT UP on two people sitting in comfortable chairs, facing each other. One is the HOST of an interview show, the other is SIR THORNAN THORNAN.

The host turns to the audience.

HOST. *Sir Thornan Thornan, president of the Strovian Mountain Council, is with us today.*

She turns and faces Sir Thornan.

HOST. *Sir Thornan Thornan, I can only begin to imagine what the past few days have been like for you. Can you help us put this recent tragedy in context?*

THORNAN. *I cannot stress enough the shame this incident has brought on all of us. Generations of Strovians have explored far and wide across the face of the earth without one single life lost. Never. Not one. It is an esteemed lineage we have inherited. All throughout the world we are known for our attention to detail and our exacting standards of safety and excellence. Every time someone hears a flight attendant say 'crosscheck and all call' humanity has us, Strovians, to thank for this invaluable contribution to airline safety.*

HOST. *Do you think Strovia can regain its status as the premier mountaineering nation in the world? What would it take? Could it happen in our lifetime?*

THORNAN. *As painful as it is to admit, I just don't know. What I do know is that it would take something so extraordinary, a feat so spectacular and singular that the entire world would have to take notice...*

LIGHT UP on two deck chairs on the opposite side of the stage. Moot sits in one, empty cans lined up on the arm of the chair. He's staring off into the distance. Lost. Sad.

Helene walks in. *That* Helene, Wilvis' teacher. She's pregnant. And weary.

HELENE. *How long?*
MOOT. *How long what?*
HELENE. *How long will you sit here and let the mountain win?*
MOOT. *The mountain didn't win. I lost.*

Helene sits down next to him. She's done with his self pity.

HELENE. *We've been through this a thousand times. I get it. Something happened and people died. But this is how you make it better? Sitting here, day after day, staring off into the distance, thinking about that mountain...*
MOOT. *You have a better idea?*
HELENE. *Do I have a better idea??? Me? I married Mootis Hermanicus Vulner the 12th! That man doesn't wait for other*

*people to have ideas. He sees something-something other
people don't see-and then he goes after it-*
MOOT. *You don't understand. It's not that simple.*

SINGLE LIGHT on Helene.

HELENE. *I DO UNDERSTAND and IT IS that simple. What do you
see Mootis my man? What do you see that no one else sees?
What's possible? What hasn't been done yet? What do you see
my love?*

LIGHT DOWN on Helene.
SINGLE LIGHT UP on Moot sitting in front of his tent. He removes
three bullets from his bag. He holds them up and inspects them
as he loads his gun.

LIGHT DOWN on Moot.
SINGLE LIGHT UP on Nella, who has taken two legs off her table
and is screwing them together end to end.

LIGHT DOWN on Nella.
LIGHT UP on two lounge chairs. A MAN walks in wearing a very
small pair of swim trunks. He surveys the audience as if they are
a breathtaking view, and then lets out a long, relaxed exhale like
he's king of the world. He sits down in one of the chairs. He's
holding a glass of champagne. Nella walks in wearing a robe over
her swimsuit, holding a glass of champagne as well. They clink
their glasses. Nella sits down.
A phone on the small table between them rings.
The man answers.
He listens for a bit.

MAN. *It is?...he did?...he what?...how?...where?...wow...OK.*

He hangs up.
He turns to Nella.

MAN. *It's out.*
NELLA. *Out?*
MAN. *Us.*
NELLA. *Us?*

MAN. *Yes. You and me. This.*
NELLA. *Our secret?*
MAN. *Our secret.*
NELLA. *Says who?*
MAN. *Says the royal press secretary. The Daily Flave just posted.*
NELLA. *Posted what?*
MAN. *A photo.*
NELLA. *A photo of what?*
MAN. *Us. On this balcony. Yesterday.*
NELLA. *But you repeatedly assured me that we are perfectly hidden here. What about all the precautions and decoy vehicles and me wearing a wig-*
MAN. *Apparently no one anticipated that a man would paint himself blue and float in the ocean for three days on a piece of foam with a long, long lens trained on this very balcony.*

They contemplate this in silence.

NELLA. *That's actually quite impressive.*
MAN. *Agreed.*
NELLA. *Does the Queen know?*

The phone rings.
The man answers.
He listens.
Ho hangs up.

MAN. *She knows.*

LIGHT DOWN on the man and Nella.
LIGHT UP on SWAYNE WAVERS, a popular Flaveyon talk show host. He's sitting at his desk on set. Next to his desk is a couch for his guests.

A STAGEHAND stands in front of Swayne's desk and addresses the audience.

STAGEHAND. *All right, we good? Third segment. Ready everyone? Here we go: Five...four...three...two...*

Stagehand holds up an APPLAUSE sign.

SWAYNE. *All right, welcome back to the show. Wow! You are a great crowd tonight, must be something in the water. Now my next guest has been on the show many, many times over the years and I have to tell you that most of the time when she's with us and she's telling us another one of her stories about traveling to an exotic location and having another incredible adventure I'm totally enthralled...but I also have this little voice in the back of my head that often wonders 'Is she winding me up? Did that really happen?'*

Stagehand holds up a LAUGH sign.

SWAYNE. *Nevertheless, I can't get enough. From mountains, to oceans, to far away lands, to your little brother, her conquests have made her a household name. Please welcome to the show the guest who only needs one name...NELLA!!!*

Nella comes out in some sort of rubber dress. She looks ridiculous. And fantastic.

NELLA. *So good to be back, Swayne! Hello everybody!*

She has clearly done this a thousand times.
She takes a seat on the couch.

SWAYNE. *You know every time you come on I have to ask what you've been up to because you always blow my mind. So tell us, what's new?*
NELLA. *Well Swayne, this year has been one for the ages. I was just in this tiny village two clicks past Zinia in the Foomarza province filming my new show and I'm holding a baby panda in one arm and a baby koala in the other when this old woman comes into the hut. She's got no teeth and a necklace made out of bones around her neck and this little monkey on her shoulder that's eating an avocado and she says 'Are you busy right now? Because a baby dragon has just been born in the next village over...would you like to hold it?'*
SWAYNE. *Ok, ok. Nella, I love this story. I really do. And I'm sure it only gets more amazing. But I have to ask before you go any further, what have you been up to?*

NELLA. *Uhhhhhh…excuse me? I was just telling you a story about a baby dragon!!!*

She looks to her right and left, to the audience for help. She's very confused.

SWAYNE. *You know what I'm asking about.*
NELLA. *I do?*
SWAYNE. *EVERYONE is talking about it. You know this right? You have to know this. So before we go any further, let's talk about it.*
NELLA. *I'm sorry, I feel like I missed something. Was this in the production notes? The panda…the koala…the dragon-*
SWAYNE. *Oh…please, Nella-the photos!*
NELLA. *I don't have photos of the panda with me. Or the dragon…*

Swayne is exasperated.

SWAYNE. *The photos…of you and the king!!!*
NELLA. *Ah yes, those.*

She would rather be anywhere else in the world right now.

SWAYNE. *That's all you have to say?*
NELLA. *Well…I…I…I believe that it's important for our private lives to remain private…*

She desperately hopes this is enough. It isn't.

SWAYNE. *Honestly Nella, are you going to tell me-tell us-that those photos are private?*
NELLA. *I prefer to respect the King and his personal life.*
SWAYNE. *Fair enough. You're going to dodge the question. I get it. But I have another question: Doesn't the perception bother you?*
NELLA. *And what would that perception be?*
SWAYNE. *Oh my, you really don't get it, do you? You are more known now for your 'relationship' with the King than for any of your accomplishments.*
NELLA. *I vigorously dispute that claim. My accomplishments speak for themselves. My personal life in no way detracts from*

my long history of record-breaking achievements…it has nothing to do with…

She trails off.

SWAYNE. *Really? You believe that? Let's try something, shall we?*

Nella half nods. She has no idea what he has in mind.
SINGLE LIGHT on Swayne.

SWAYNE. *You the audience-let me ask you a question: How many of you know of Nella because of her 'record breaking achievements?'*

A thin smattering of applause.

SWAYNE. *Interesting. Now, how many of you know of her only as the woman rumored to be shagging our beloved King?*

Stagehand raises the APPLAUSE sign.

LIGHT DOWN on Swayne.
LIGHT UP up on Nella, sitting at her tent. As she attaches two legs of her table together, she slides off an outer sheath revealing that the legs together form a SPEAR. She holds it up and thrusts it forward like you'd do if you were trying to kill someone.

LIGHT DOWN on Nella.
LIGHT UP on Reesh. He's walking toward REGGIE FANG, his agent, who's standing in among four padded chairs. Sitting in the other two chairs are LOUIS ORTAN, his accountant, and SHEILA LEELA, his manager.

REESH. *Reggie! My agent calls and I am there! My ninja sense tells me you got something big for me or you wouldn't have wanted me to come in-am I right or am I right?*
REGGIE. *It is definitely big, you got that right. Thanks so much for coming in Reesh…*

Reesh sees the other two and is instantly on edge.

REESH. *Hey…Louis…and Sheila….I didn't know you two were going to be here…*

He looks at Reggie nervously. He's trying not to appear rattled.

REESH. *Reggie didn't tell me-*
REGGIE. *I didn't. You're right. Listen, Reesh, I don't want you to feel like you walked into a trap but I knew if I told you who was going to be here you'd probably not come-*
LOUIS. *So we're not going to waste your time. There are a few things that as your accountant-*
SHEILA. *And as your manager-*
LOUIS. *We need to tell you. And you can do whatever you want with them.*

Reesh drops into one of the chairs reluctantly.

REESH. *I feel like I'm in an intervention or something.*
SHEILA. *That's a word for it.*
REGGIE. *Bottom line, Reesh: You're about to be in serious financial trouble.*
REESH. *About to be? But what about all the new-*
LOUIS. *Tell you what, let me explain. We're three or four weeks away from your losses and expenses exceeding your income and assets. At that point you will go into debt. And that debt will get very big, very fast because those loans have a lot of interest on them.*
REESH. *Well of course they have a lot of interest, a lot of people are very interested in me.*

Louis glances at Reggie and Sheila.

LOUIS. *No, not interest as in people being interested in you, interest as in how much you owe in addition to the principal.*
SHEILA. *Reesh, your eyes are already glazing over.*
REESH. *You guys know I'm not into all that-*
SHEILA. *Right. Let me try to explain in a way you'll understand. Imagine that you're out to dinner with seven women-*

Reesh turns to Louis.

REESH. *See? Now this I can follow!*
SHEILA. *And you want to show them a great time so you're paying for dinner. Now imagine that each woman's meal is costing you fifty dollars.*
REESH. *Does that include drinks?*
SHEILA. *Yes.*
REESH. *What about the tip?*

Louis puts his head in his hands.

LOUIS. *AHHHH! REESH!! Fifty dollars a person. Not complicated. Includes tip!*
REESH. *Pump the brakes there, Louis, just asking. Proceed, Sheila.*
SHEILA. *So if there are seven of them, then the bill is going to be seven women times the fifty dollars for each meal which is going to be three hundred and fifty dollars total. Got it?*
REESH. *What about me?*
SHEILA. *What about you?*
REESH. *Me. What about the cost of my meal?*
SHEILA. *The owner of the restaurant is a fan of yours and your meal is on the house, how's that?*

Reesh nods to Louis.

REESH. *Once again, I can grasp THAT.*
SHEILA. *So you're out three hundred and fifty dollars. It's an expense, something you did have but now you don't have it. Now, stay with me here. Imagine if during the meal you sold seven of your BARE-CHESTED, BABY! action figures.*
REESH. *Together?*
REGGIE. *Together? What do you mean?*
REESH. *Yeah, together. Did they come to my website together or was it seven different women who don't know each other?*
REGGIE. *You lost me-*
REESH. *Did I sell seven action figures to one woman or did seven different women each buy one action figure?*
LOUIS. *Now why would that even matter?*
REESH. *Oh man Louis, these are exactly the things that matter.*
SHEILA. *They don't know each other. Seven random women*

from all over the world, and they each purchase an action figure of you for fifty dollars.
REESH. *The first edition or the collector's edition with the Real Gold Sash?*

He says REAL GOLD SASH like it's the coolest thing ever.

SHEILA. *The one that costs fifty dollars. Stay with me here, because this is my point: if that happens you have spent three hundred and fifty dollars during dinner but you have also made three hundred and fifty dollars during dinner so it's a wash. You're back to zero. The same went out that came in.*
REESH. *Got it.*
LOUIS. *Which brings us to the present. With taxes and expenditures and a number of invoices that are past due-let alone your monthly expenses-we're about to reach the point where you have the same amount coming in that you have going out. And then, when we pass that point, you'll have MORE going out than is coming IN-*
REGGIE. *Which is called debt-*
LOUIS. *And debt is serious. Really serious.*
REESH. *But what about Macho Nachos? People stop me on the street all the time to tell me how much they love them.*
SHEILA. *Well...yes...about Macho Nachos. It's important to understand that somebody stopping you in public to tell you they like something from your frozen food product line-I can only imagine that's thrilling for you-but it's not an accurate way to measure whether or not a new product launch is successful. Because what we've learned is that the larger market simply isn't trending towards nachos with rabbit meat-*
REGGIE. *Which brings us to a larger issue that we're seeing across the board. In this case, what the data is telling us is that the real issue has more to do with the word 'macho.'*
REESH. *That's a great word! How could anybody-I LOVE that word!*
REGGIE. *Which is the problem. When you say the word you say it with a straight face. Like you mean it.*
REESH. *Like I mean it? Isn't that the point of words-and talking?*
REGGIE. *Well yes...it is. But that's not the-tell you what, let me show you something. Do this. Say the word 'macho.'*
REESH. *Macho.*

REGGIE. *See?*
REESH. *See what?*
REGGIE. *See how you don't say it ironically?*

Reesh doesn't understand what Reggie's saying.

SHEILA. *Let's come at this from a different angle. Louis, repeat after me: 'I am a macho man.'*
LOUIS. *I am a macho man.*
SHEILA. *Reesh, can you see how Louis can't keep a straight face when he says it, how he can't say it seriously?*
REESH. *That's because he's not a macho man.*
SHEILA. *Now you, Reggie, you say it.*
REGGIE. *I am a macho man.*

Reggie can't keep a straight face either.

SHEILA. *Do you see how neither of them can take themselves seriously when they use that word?*
REESH. *No, I don't see what you're-*
SHEILA. *THIS is the problem, Reesh. The world has changed. And you can't see it.*
REGGIE. *Which leads us to the truth behind the truth: All these revenue streams, from food to your clothing line to the workout equipment to your candle and bed linen line-it's all based on something you did. Something in the past. A desert you hiked through, a sea you rowed across-*
REESH. *A mountain I mounted.*
REGGIE. *There you go, a mountain you mounted. Exactly-*
LOUIS. *But it's been seven years since you did anything new.*
SHEILA. *Listen, Reesh, times have changed. Doing everything without wearing a shirt, that had its moment. But those days are over.*
LOUIS. *And if we don't start off-loading assets quickly you're going to be in serious financial trouble, and it's our job to protect you from that.*
REESH. *Why didn't you tell me any of this sooner?*
REGGIE. *We did. We have. We tried. For the past three years, those times I called you and said we needed to talk, this is what we needed to talk about.*
SHEILA. *Those spreadsheets I emailed you-*

REESH. *But you should have said-*
LOUIS. *SAID WHAT??? WE DID!!! How much louder could we have yelled? How many more times could we have said we need to show you some things?*

Sheila holds up her phone.

SHEILA. *Here's one: I sent you the first quarter Macho Nachos numbers and you sent me back this text:*

Reesh reads it off her phone.

REESH. *Let's float down the river together on this one...*

He turns to the three of them.

REESH. *That's deep.*
LOUIS. *Reesh, we're here today to tell you there is no river.*
SHEILA. *And you are not floating, you're sinking. Fast.*

Silence for a beat.

REGGIE. *Unless...*

He nods to Louis.

LOUIS. *Unless...*
REESH. *Unless I do something new.*

Reesh gets up from his chair and starts walking across the stage to his tent.

REESH. *And not just new-massive. Unprecedented. Something that puts me right back in the middle of the action. Something that people can't help but talk about. Something that isn't about THEN, it's about NOW. Something no one has ever done before...*

SINGLE LIGHT on Reesh at his tent, where he takes apart the straps that held the tombstone to his back and pulls out wires, which are attached to wooden handles, the kind you'd grip if you snuck up behind someone to strangle them.

LIGHT FADES on the peak.
Chorus 2 moves the MOON on the end of his pole across the stage. Night.

All four climbers can be seen in front of their tents with their various weapons.
Chorus 1 walks to the front of the stage.

CHORUS 1. *And so we reach the end of DAY ONE. Four climbers, from four different nations, all going to sleep thinking the exact same thing:*
ALL FOUR TOGETHER. *Tomorrow, I'm going to have to KILL THEM ALL.*

LIGHTS OUT.

DAY TWO.

FLICKERS OF LIGHT.
A brief bit of music.
LIGHTS UP on the peak.

Chorus 2 comes out on the far right side of the stage with the
Sun on a pole. Morning.

We hear the sound of a **FUSE** being lit, and then a BANG! as a
banner unfurls. It reads: **DAY TWO.**

All four climbers sit in front of their tents, stretching and yawning
like you do when you first wake up.

A MAN casually strolls onto the peak. He's wearing a wind-
breaker, jeans, and running shoes. He has a small bag over his
shoulder.

He looks around, admiring the view.
He notices the other four.
His name is GARY SMITH.

GARY SMITH. *Hey guys! How's it going?*

They can't believe what they're seeing.

GARY SMITH. *Beautiful morning, isn't it? And that view!!!
It just doesn't get old. WOW. Say it backwards: WOW!*

They slowly begin to stand.

GARY SMITH. *So what are you guys doing up here? Wait, let me
guess: A bunch of buddies camping for the weekend? Nooooo…
hold on-don't tell me. Is this a bachelor party? Is one of you
getting hitched? Because this view would make you want to find
a special someone and settle down, how could you not be feeling
those feelings???!!!*

They're slowly gathering around him, mesmerized.

GARY SMITH. *Ha! And you spent the night up here?! WOOOO!!! Danger be thy middle name!!! Some people live on the edge!!!*
THART PALLS. *Enough with the jibber jabber!!! Who are you?*
GARY SMITH. *Oh, yes, sorry-so rude of me! I'm Gary Smith. Great to meet you. And your name is-*
THART PALLS. *Gary Smith?*
GARY SMITH. *It was when I left! And you are...?*
THART PALLS. *Thart Palls.*
GARY SMITH. *Fart Balls? That's awesome!*
THART PALLS. *Palls. Thart Palls.*
GARY SMITH. *Well that's doing some fancy grammar gymnastics right there. Imagine if 'Palls' was a verb-maybe it is...your name could be a sentence: Thart Palls. He does? He palls? Thart Palls? How often? Words. Names. Verbs. Nouns. Aren't they amazing?*
REESH. *Greetings my good man, I see that you too have triumphed over this most arduous of climbs.*
GARY SMITH. *Actually, it was surprisingly invigorating. Nothing like a few of those inclines on the way up to get the ol' blood pumping.*
REESH. *I am Reeshafesh Soontamgamonous Milepheshar-*
GARY SMITH. *That's a...what? Should I know what that is? Is it contagious?*
REESH. *It's my name-*
NELLA. *And I am Nella, from the great land of Flaveyon.*
GARY SMITH. *A real life Flaveyon? Am I dreaming? Someone pinch me with a clip from a bag of chips! Are you kidding me? A Flaveyon? In flesh and blood? This is so cool.*
REESH. *And I am a Xilnan.*

He bows.
Gary Smith returns the bow, utterly fascinated.

GARY SMITH. *I have no idea what you just said but I feel like we've got quite a thing going here, you and me.*
MOOT. *I'm Moot Vulner, a Strovian through and through, born and raised.*
GARY SMITH. *Guys!!! This is so fantabulous! You're all from different countries???!!! What are the odds of that? Other countries....that is just tremendous. Different foods and clothes and music and words-man, people being from other places is just the best.*

Thart Palls is so suspicious.

THART PALLS. *Well, isn't this pleasant. Now before we all join hands and sing together I have some questions-*
GARY SMITH. *NO WAY!!! You guys SING TOGETHER??? Well of course you do!!! How could you not want to sing in a place like this?*
THART PALLS. *No, no. Not singing. Questions. We have questions. What are you doing here?*
GARY SMITH. *Honestly Mr. Hall Carts-*
THART PALLS. *Palls! Thart Palls.*
GARY SMITH. *Bart Z. Falls...I don't understand the question-*

Gary Smith is interrupted by Chorus 1 who brings out the bird on the pole. He moves it in circles above their heads. Gary Smith goes slack-jawed.

GARY SMITH. *WHOOOAAAHHHHHHHH. OHHHHHHHHHH. WWWWOOOOWWWWW...*

He spreads out his arms slowly like he's trying to squeeze every last ounce out of this moment with this bird.

GARY SMITH. *That is sooooooo beautiful...How do you...How do you see...THAT...and not think there's a whole world right here within this one?*

A long pause.
He returns from wherever he was.

GARY SMITH. *Oh that's right, you were asking something?*
THART PALLS. *I was. What is your angle? Your plan, your scheme, your...thing? Why are you HERE?*
GARY SMITH. *This? Oh man. If I told you, you wouldn't believe me. You people in your fancy outfits with your hi-tech equipment, you're on another level from a wanderin' willy like me.*
MOOT. *You aren't a climber?*
THART PALLS. *Of course he's a climber, he got up here!*
GARY SMITH. *Ha! Me a climber!? That's a good one. No, this is all totally new to me. I've never done this before.*
MOOT. *This is the first mountain you've climbed?*

GARY SMITH. *Climbed? This is the first mountain I've ever been on!*
THART PALLS. *There's something really dodgy about all this, something you're not telling us.*
GARY SMITH. *Thart Palls you salty dog, you. THAT is funny, 'something dodgy about me.' You want to know why I'm here?*
THART PALLS. *Yes, absolutely. We demand it.*
GARY SMITH. *Well, all right then-but can we sit down or something? My legs turned to JELLO about half a click back...*

They arrange some blankets and sleeping bags and end up sitting in a circle, like you do in school for second grade story time.

GARY SMITH. *I'm a school teacher. Seventh grade. Reading and writing, mostly.*

SINGLE LIGHT on Gary Smith. He has a stapler in one hand and a trash can in the other. He steps up on a chair and sings, opera style.

GARY SMITH. *Thousands of aliens are attacking the school!!! Who will diagram the sentence on the board to repel their attack and set us free so we can live in peace? And get ten extra credit points for saving humanity?*

LIGHT SHIFTS and Gary Smith is back sitting with them.

GARY SMITH. *That sort of thing.*
NELLA. *You're a school teacher?*

LIGHT SHIFTS again. Now he's holding a clicker like you do when you're giving a presentation.

GARY SMITH. *First, there was vinyl, then 8 track. Then cassettes, then CD's, then MP3's-PAY ATTENTION PEOPLE! This will be on the test.*

LIGHT SHIFTS and he's back.

GARY SMITH. *Yeah, I'm a teacher. You're looking like you don't*

know what I'm talking about. You know what a teacher is, right?
NELLA. *Of course. We Flaveyons have the best schools in the world.*
GARY SMITH. *Well, I don't know about that Ms. Nella. But I do know that I love it. Just finished my ninth year. Can you believe it? All those young minds, so impressionable-and I get them for six hours a day. Six hours a day! What a job!*
THART PALLS. *Yeah great, whatever. But get to it. You're here. YOU MADE IT UP HERE!!! We need some answers.*
GARY SMITH. *Who peed in your sweet tea there fella? You're sure wound a bit tight...got your shorts in a bunch about something.*
REESH. *That he does, broseph. That he does. But do continue.*
GARY SMITH. *All right then, I'll tell you. Over the past few years I began to notice something with my students. When I talk about concepts or principles or abstract ideas their eyes glaze over. They drift off, they stare out the window. I lose them. But then I tell a story and BOOM!!!! They come to life. They are plugged in. It's like flipping a switch.*

He does that motion like you're flipping a switch. We hear the click.

LIGHTS SHIFT to SINGLE LIGHT on Gary Smith, sitting on a stool talking to the audience like they're his students.

GARY SMITH. *And then I take the statue out of my bag and I hold it in front of the dog. And mind you-it hasn't eaten in two days and it's baring its teeth at me and there's drool and slobber coming out the sides of its mouth. I begin to slowly move the statue back and forth as I lock eyes on the beast. I tell him how sleepy he is, isn't he? I tell him he's feeling drowsy and tired and he'd like to lie down in the dirt right now and take a nap, wouldn't he? And then he begins to move his head back and forth, following the statue with those piercing canine eyes, and honestly for the first time, I start to think that I'm going to live to tell about this...*

LIGHT SHIFTS to Gary Smith back with the others.

GARY SMITH. *I'm telling you, if all I'm talking about is just facts*

and figures, it's like pushing a hill up a rock-
NELLA. *Isn't the expression 'pushing a rock up a hill?'*
GARY SMITH. *Well now, I don't know how you Flaveyons do it, but have you ever tried to push a HILL up something? It's exhausting-*
REESH. *Please, continue your tale.*
GARY SMITH. *Oh yes, right. Now here's the thing I began to realize this past year: I don't have enough stories. And the ones I do have, I've told so many times it's gotten to the point where I'll launch into one I've told before and they'll immediately stop me and say 'GARY SMITH WE'VE ALREADY HEARD THIS ONE!' You just can't repeat yourself in this game, know what I mean? So I decided I had to go out and get some new stories.*
MOOT. *I don't follow. 'Go out and get some new stories?'*
GARY SMITH. *Yes. I decided that the problem is I HAVEN'T LIVED AN INTERESTING ENOUGH LIFE. That's why I don't have that many stories. So, when school was out this year I decided to go find some stories.*
NELLA. *So you climbed this mountain?*
GARY SMITH. *Yep. You gotta start somewhere. Baby steps, right? I was sitting there one day in the pub with my friend Simon-*

Gary Smith crosses the stage to where SIMON sits on a stool. Gary Smith sits down on the stool next to him.

GARY SMITH. *And I was telling Simon how I need to get some new stories and Simon said-*
SIMON. *Well, you could always climb a mountain.*
GARY SMITH. *And I said 'That's a good idea, Simon. Do you want to come with me?' And he said*
SIMON. *No. I have a dentist appointment and then I have to paint my fence.*
GARY SMITH. *And then I said 'I don't remember you having a fence.' And then Simon said*
SIMON. *That's why I have to paint it.*

Gary Smith leaves the pub and gets on a bike, talking as he rides to the other side of the stage.

GARY SMITH. *So I came alone.*

SINGLE LIGHT UP on a restaurant booth. DONNA, Gary Smith's fiancé, sits waiting. Gary Smith sets his bike down and joins her in the booth.

GARY SMITH. *Hey babe, sorry I'm late.*

She's glued to her phone, refusing to look him in the eyes.

DONNA. *Twenty seven minutes?*
GARY SMITH. *I know, I know. I apologize. It's totally my fault. I just didn't count on so much of it being uphill.*

Now she looks up.

DONNA. *Uphill?*

Gary Smith immediately regrets saying this.

GARY SMITH. *Oh…that's nothing, just a little miscalculation on my part-*
DONNA. *Uphill? What do you mean by uphill?*
GARY SMITH. *I rode my bike here.*

He says it like it's a deep, dark confession.

GARY SMITH. *It took longer than I thought it would.*
DONNA. *Why didn't you come like a normal human in your car?*

Now it's Gary Smith's turn to look down.

GARY SMITH. *I don't have my car anymore.*
DONNA. *What? Why? What happened TO YOUR CAR?*

She spits fire. It is not pleasant to witness.

GARY SMITH. *I sold it.*
DONNA. *Wait. This doesn't have anything to do with…oh please help me if it does…this isn't at all by any chance connected to your little-*
GARY SMITH. *It is. And it does.*
DONNA. *You sold your car to pay for your little vacation?*

Acid dripping from her words.

GARY SMITH. *It's not a 'little vacation.' It's important. I have to do it.*

It is all she can do to contain her fury.

DONNA. *HAVE TO DO IT??? You have to do it??? When you first started talking about your little trippy trip I would tell myself 'OH DONNA, just let him get it out of his system. It's not like he's ever going to follow through and actually do it.' BUT YOU ARE!!! You're going to leave me for the summer??? And then you sit here and tell me that it's something YOU HAVE TO DO. Well you know what I have to do??? I have to explain to my parents why we won't be coming to the lake house in July. Imagine how difficult that is going to be.*
GARY SMITH. *You can still go to the lake house.*

As soon as he says it he realizes he just poured gas on the fire.

DONNA. *Alone??? Without you??? Me and my parents-and you're not there???!!! How would I ever explain to anybody where you were and why I was alone? Do you realize the situation this puts me in? We've gone to the lake house TOGETHER for the past seven summers! And now suddenly I'm there alone?*
GARY SMITH. *People go places alone all the time.*
DONNA. *I feel like I don't even know you anymore! HOW IS IT EVEN SUMMER IF WE DON'T GO TO THE LAKE HOUSE?*
GARY SMITH. *Not to point out the obvious here, but you'd have to have a lake house to even know to ask that question.*

A WAITER approaches the table.

WAITER. *You guys ready to order?*
DONNA. *NO!!!!!*

LIGHT DOWN on Donna.
LIGHT UP on the other side of the stage on RON MONTALBAN, a teacher from Gary Smith's school.
He's sitting on the bench seat of a car, resting his hands on a steering wheel. He's blasting Lady Gaga.

RON. *Gary Smith my boooooooyyyyyy. What you doin' walkin' to school? Hop in!*

Gary Smith sits down next to him.

GARY SMITH. *Hey Ron. The Gaga? First thing in the morning?*
RON. *You got it! Few things will get a man more in the mood to reveal the mysteries of mechanical physics to sophomores than the GAGA HERSELF.*
GARY SMITH. *That's a sentence no one has ever said in the history of the world.*
RON. *Says the English teacher! Man, you know your stuff. By the way, where's your car?*
GARY SMITH. *I've been riding my bike to work lately. You know, exercise and all that.*
RON. *Soooooo…where's your bike?*
GARY SMITH. *I didn't ride it today.*
RON. *So why didn't you drive?*
GARY SMITH. *You just don't let up, do you? I don't have my car anymore. I sold it.*
RON. *Ahhh yes, the old 'in between.' I got you. Been there myself. So many options out there-you thinkin' of doing something radical like gettin' a hybrid?*
GARY SMITH. *Oh, it's not like that. I sold my car to pay for my trip.*
RON. *A trip? That is awesome. Where you going?*
GARY SMITH. *Hiking.*
RON. *Hiking. I dig it. Where?*
GARY SMITH. *Kind of all over.*

LIGHTS OUT on Ron and Gary Smith.
SINGLE LIGHT up on LINDA MEANDA, a math teacher at the school. She's standing next to the water cooler in the teachers' lounge. As she begins to speak Ron and Gary Smith appear at her side.

LINDA. *What am I doing this summer? Well, this might just blow your mind, because it's going to get crazy around our place. Cliff-you all know Cliff, right?-he's in the process of installing a flat screen television above our hot tub on the back patio. We love the show NCIS. It's just so riveting and the episodes are so* *different from each other and you just never know how it's going to turn out. We figured out that to watch every episode of every season would take two hundred and thirty seven hours. And then we realized that if we watch three episodes a night in our hot tub we could see every single episode in one summer with the series finale the night before school starts. How wild is that gonna be?*

Gary Smith is so bored.

GARY SMITH. *Wow, that is quite a goal.*
LINDA. *I know Gary Smith, trust me I KNOW. Like I always tell my students-*

SINGLE LIGHT on Linda.

LINDA. *You don't know what you're capable of until you try. You gotta put your mind to it and get focused and get out there and have some adventures!!!*

LIGHT DOWN on Linda.
LIGHT UP on Gary Smith sitting in a plastic chair next to a large sign that reads YARD SALE. Ron laughs as he walks up.

RON. *So I'm at Costco and I run into Phyllis-she teaches freshman trigonometry, you know her-anyway, she tells me she's just driven by your place and it looked like you had all your earthly possessions laid out in your front yard. And upon further inspection, I do believe her assessment was accurate. Of course I had to see for myself. Listen man, are you okay? Do you need to see the school counsellor? This trip thing you're going on-has it gone to your head?*
GARY SMITH. *Nah. I'm doing fine Ron-*
RON. *But seriously, Gary Smith, is this what I think it is? Are you selling your stuff to pay for your hike?*
GARY SMITH. *Pretty much.*

LIGHTS DOWN on Gary Smith and Ron.
LIGHTS UP on the mountain. All four climbers are standing, facing each other. Gary Smith returns to where he was talking to them.

THART PALLS. *Stories?*
MOOT. *Stories?*
NELLA. *Stories?*
REESH. *Stories?*
GARY SMITH. *Yeah, stories.*
THART PALLS. *You climbed this mountain so you could get new stories?*
GARY SMITH. *Well, I don't know if this answers your question Señor Tharte, but I did see a family of knuckas.*
REESH. *What? You saw knuckas?*
GARY SMITH. *A whole family of them.*
MOOT. *You're joking.*
GARY SMITH. *Nope. With my own two eyes.*
NELLA. *But knuckas don't exist. That's been agreed upon by everyone, am I correct?*
THART PALLS. *That is correct. Same with unicorns and yetis and other fictional creatures that rational human beings with functioning brains all know ARE NOT REAL.*
GARY SMITH. *Well I don't know about that, but I saw a family of them.*

Moot is dumbfounded.
They all are.

MOOT. *Allow me to suspend all logic and reason for a moment. WHERE did you see this family of knuckas?*
GARY SMITH. *Oh man, it was incredible. There was this huge open plain part way up the mountain with this cliff at one end and a grove of pine trees at the other. It took forever to cross it and then I reached this river with these square shaped rocks-*
NELLA. *Excuse me, I hate to hit the pause button, but were those rocks covered in green moss? And was there a waterfall up and to the right?*
GARY SMITH. *Yes! Exactly! That's the place-*
NELLA. *That's the route I took!!! And to think-*
GARY SMITH. *That wasn't the only place I saw knuckas.*
REESH. *You saw them more than once?*
GARY SMITH. *More than once? Ha! I witnessed a knucka mid-shed!!!*

A gasp from Nella.

MOOT. *Now you're just making things up. The whole knucka shedding thing is a myth, right?*
GARY SMITH. *Well, now, Mr. Sir Mootis, I do not know about that but I did witness a knucka mid-shed.*
NELLA. *Positively astonishing. Do tell what you saw.*
GARY SMITH. *He was on a branch. About twenty feet up. Just a little fella. And he'd clamped those little knucka feet to the bark like his furry little life depended on it-*
REESH. *Yes! This is exactly how I have heard it described-*
THART PALLS. *In a book of fairy tales.*
GARY SMITH. *I'd been watching him for at least an hour or two when he squeezes his eyes shut so tight I thought they were going to pop out of his skull. I just froze there. I didn't move a muscle. Because suddenly I thought to myself 'Is this a mid-shed? Am I actually witnessing a mid-shed?' I'm telling you-*

Nella loses her cool.

NELLA. *Oh how thrilling! My heart would have burst a valve!*

The others turn to her.
She collects herself.

NELLA. *Do go on.*
GARY SMITH. *And then...poof...*
NELLA. *Poof?*
REESH. *Poof?*
MOOT. *Poof?*
THART PALLS. *What's a poof?*
REESH. *You know not of the POOF on Rogol-Fogol?*
GARY SMITH. *Wait-you're from Rogol-Fogol? That's a real place that people are from? How did I miss that? Far out! King Lisp and all that! Wait til I tell my friends back home I met someone from Rogol-Fogol. They will not believe me-*
THART PALLS. *Yes, it's a real place. But apparently a place that failed to educate people like me on what a POOF is.*
GARY SMITH. *A poof is like a...sheesh, it's hard to explain...a poof is like a contained explosion. Like a nonviolent detonation. A poof is like witnessing something being blown into a million bits and yet in the very same second it transmits an indestructible sense of peace and calm.*

NELLA. *Well said, Gary Smith.*
REESH. *He is a teacher of language and writing.*
MOOT. *So there's the poof. Then what happens to the knucka?*
GARY SMITH. *His hair falls out.*
MOOT. *Just like that?*
GARY SMITH. *Just like that. No noise. No movement. No faint rustle. His hair was attached to his body. And then it wasn't.*
REESH. *Where'd it go?*
GARY SMITH. *That's the bizarre part-*
THART PALLS. *That's the bizarre part???!!! That? The rest was perfectly reasonable, but that's-*
GARY SMITH. *Some of it blew away in the wind. Although there was no wind, know what I'm sayin'? And some of it fell down to the ground. Although when I checked the ground I couldn't find any. And the rest of it-I was watching so carefully-the rest of it...disappeared.*
MOOT. *No way.*

Moot whispers this. Like a child. It's charming.

GARY SMITH. *Yes way, Captain Hermanicus. I just stood there, looking that little fella in the eyes. All naked there on that branch. All alone. And his skin, his skin was this translucent gray with just a hint of silver. I can't find the words for it. But his eyes weren't bulging anymore. So that was nice. And I bet he had a clear view of those geysers from up there.*
MOOT. *Geysers?*
GARY SMITH. *Did I leave that part out? There must have been a hundred of them. At least. Super eerie. They made this ominous hissing sound. The whole area smelled like mayonnaise. Mixed with gym socks. And beans.*
REESH. *Brief inquiry if you don't mind: was there by any chance an area of quicksand on the other side of that geyser field?*
GARY SMITH. *So that's what that was!!! I couldn't figure it out. I dropped a cool looking rock I'd found along the way and when I went back to pick it up it was gone. Now I know what happened: quicksand.*
REESH. *Was there a river nearby that split into three streams just past that quicksand area?*
GARY SMITH. *Yes!!! Wow, you ask the best questions. How'd you know?*

THART PALLS. *Because that's the route he took!!!*

Reesh nods.

GARY SMITH. *Oh man, you guys are just the best! First,
I just happen to stumble upon your super cool camp. What are
the odds of that? And then I find out that we took the same
routes up the mountain. I love it that you're all into my knucka
stories, you're the first people I've gotten to tell them to-*
THART PALLS. *Hold on. You have more stories? You saw more
knuckas-that don't exist-than just the ones you've told us about?*
GARY SMITH. *I saw so many I lost track and stopped counting.
Sometimes it felt as if they were everywhere. LIKE HOW COULD
YOU NOT SEE THEM? Like the mountain was covered in them. I
was strolling once in the evening, it must have been a month or
so ago-I've had a hard time keeping track of time while I've been
away. The sun was setting and I saw a group of them walking
along the ridge of a hill.*
NELLA. *I read somewhere that the mother doesn't go first, the
youngest goes first, then the mother, then the rest-is that true?*
GARY SMITH. *Well that explains it! Because the sun was back
lighting them in such a way that I could just see their outlines and
that's when I realized-*
REESH. *KNUCKLE!!!*

Gary Smith gives Reesh a fist bump.

GARY SMITH. *Exactly! Knuckle, brother.*
MOOT. *I missed something.*
NELLA. *This is straight from ancient knucka lore. It's been said
that when you see a family of knuckas on a ridge they make the
shape of your knuckles.*

She holds up her fist and then turns it towards Moot, who holds
up his fist in the same way.

MOOT. *Knuckles. Knuckas.*
GARY SMITH. *The best.*
MOOT. *There was a ridge?*
GARY SMITH. *Oh man that section on the way up was sooooo
loopy. The ridge started up top as a cliff and then just kept*

angling down until it was this long steep incline with all these boulders strewn across it-
MOOT. *A bit like you imagine the surface of the moon?*
GARY SMITH. *Well now that you say it like that, yeah. Gray, really gray. And there was a lake-*
MOOT. *Did the water have a reddish tint to it?*
GARY SMITH. *You better believe it. How'd you know?*
MOOT. *That's the route I took up.*
THART PALLS. *Gary Smith took all three of your routes, didn't he?*
GARY SMITH. *Well I don't know about that, Mr. Thartwork in the Hall, but there's another story I think you'd enjoy.*
THART PALLS. *There's a knucka story you think I would enjoy? Really? Do go on...*
GARY SMITH. *When I was almost to the top, I came across some knuckas and I swear to you, they were building something. They were working together with these stones and piles of cones and sticks and reeds they'd collected-you hear me?-THEY WERE MAKING SOMETHING.*
MOOT. *Were the sticks chopped up?*
GARY SMITH. *No, they were smooth, like they'd been sanded down. I have no idea how they did it because obviously they don't have teeth. And they were arranging the cones in patterns of half circle shapes between a stream and a cave. That was fascinating enough, but the part I couldn't get over was that one of them was stronger than the others, and she-*
NELLA. *How did you know it was a she?*
GARY SMITH. *That's a good point. I guess she just seemed more intelligent than the others?*
MOOT. *Fair play to her.*
GARY SMITH. *Fair play to her is right-because she was giving the others directions.*
REESH. *Like a boss?*
GARY SMITH. *Like a FUZZY BOSS! And the chatter. I'm telling you, she was TALKING to them. In these short little staccato bursts of noise. LIKE A LANGUAGE.*

Gary Smith does an impression of the noise she was making.

NELLA. *I'm still unclear-what made you think she was the boss?*
GARY SMITH. *Because they would gather around her and get*

quiet and listen while she squawked and then they'd all get busy arranging and then they'd come back together and get quiet and she'd talk to them again...
REESH. *How long did this go on for?*
GARY SMITH. *Four or five, maybe six-*

Moot throws up his hands.

MOOT. *Six hours! That's incredible!!*
GARY SMITH. *No-days. Six days.*
REESH. *Six days? You just watched...?*
GARY SMITH. *I didn't move. I stood there perfectly still, barely breathing. Like I told you earlier, I HAD A HARD TIME WITH TIME IF YOU KNOW WHAT I MEAN.*
MOOT. *I have no idea what you mean.*
GARY SMITH. *It was...BENDY.*
MOOT. *WHAT was bendy?*
GARY SMITH. *Time. Like a rubber band.*
MOOT. *That doesn't help.*
GARY SMITH. *Think about your life: You wake up. You eat. You go to your job. You go to sleep. You wake up again. You have a schedule. You do this thing at this time, that thing at that time. It all moves along at a pretty steady clip, each thing taking up a certain amount of UNITS OF TIME. Minutes, hours, days...I don't even know what I'm saying here. But what happened to me that I wasn't expecting was school was out and I left but I didn't just leave my life, I left that understanding of time. Suddenly there was no schedule, no thing I had to do next, NO UNITS. Just walking.*
NELLA. *And how was that-what's the word you used?- BENDY???*
GARY SMITH. *Well, if something was interesting, I would just stop and notice. In my normal life, everything has to end. If you come across something interesting or fascinating or enjoyable, you'll have a brief taste of it and then you'll have to move on. Because it's time for the next thing. Everything ends because everything has to fit into that conception of time. THIS, THEN THAT, THEN THAT, then after THAT, THAT, THEN THAT COMES NEXT, ON and ON it goes. But those knuckas-I would see one and I'd just freeze and soak it all in. Like time didn't have the same power it normally has. Like I could let the knucka moment*

take me wherever it wanted. Man I sound like a nut bag saying this out loud...

Reesh faces Gary Smith and bows slightly.

REESH. *You were on knucka time, my brother.*
THART PALLS. *Not to interrupt here, but a quick detail question: you said all of this was happening next to a stream?*
GARY SMITH. *I did say stream but that might not be the right word for it. Because it was deep. It was only five or six feet across but I couldn't see the bottom, and the water was really clear. It was kind of spooky to be honest with you. It was more like a gash in the mountain with water in it...*
THART PALLS. *What was beside the stream-*
GARY SMITH. *I almost forgot. On both sides of the stream was this tall blue grass. And it swayed in the wind and you could lay in it and it would hold you up, like a bed, but lighter...I've never seen anything like it. And then at the edge of the grass there were-*
THART PALLS. *Big round boulders. The size of houses.*

Thart Palls shakes his head in disbelief.
Moot turns to him.

MOOT. *He took your route as well?*
THART PALLS. *He did.*
MOOT. *He took all four routes.*
THART PALLS. *He took ALL of our routes.*
GARY SMITH. *It does seem like I've been walking for a while.*
NELLA. *It's quite astonishing the more one reflects on it. He literally hiked the entire mountain...*
REESH. *And saw knuckas everywhere.*
NELLA. *That we missed.*
REESH. *Didn't see one.*

Gary Smith fumbles through his bag. He can't seem to find whatever he's looking for.

GARY SMITH. *Any chance any of you have any extra food?*

Three of them look at Moot.

ALL THREE TOGETHER. *He does.*
GARY SMITH. *Excellent…I'll look forward to a hearty breakfast in the morning because I am knackered. All that walkin' and talkin' and storytellin' has done me in.*

And with that, Gary Smith lies down on the ground and closes his eyes. The four of them stand over him, watching him fall asleep.

After several beats, they gradually make their way back to their tents, climb in, and go to sleep while Chorus 2 brings out the MOON on a pole.

Chorus 1 enters and makes her way to the front of the stage.

CHORUS 1. *And so we arrive at the end of DAY TWO.*

LIGHTS DOWN.
Trippy music plays.
LITTLE LIGHTS FLICKER.

DAY THREE.

LIGHTS UP.
We hear the sound of a fuse being lit and going off as a banner unfurls from the ceiling that reads: **DAY THREE.**

CHORUS 1. *Day three. This is the day the planes are coming.*

Chorus 1 exits.

Gary Smith sits up. He puts a few things in his bag as he stands.

GARY SMITH. *Hey guys. Morning.*

They gradually begin to stir and then sit up.

GARY SMITH. *I got a little gratitude buzz this morning, gettin' a natural high off those thankful fumes…this has been one for the ages, hasn't it? Who knew I'd run into you wild ones and make some new friends??? I feel like we really clicked! Just goes to show you never know what tomorrow might bring. Which I guess in this case was yesterday.*

They're now standing, watching him like they did when he first arrived.

GARY SMITH. *AAANYWHOOOO I'm going to need to hit the trail. Anyone know what day it is? Because school has got to be starting soon. I took my time getting up but now I got to hustle to get back. GOTTA HOOF IT! Got to get myself a SKEDADDLIN' down the mountain!*

Thart Palls has a wounded look on his face.

THART PALLS. *That's it? You're just going to leave us? Now? So suddenly?*

His voice cracks just a touch.

GARY SMITH. *Yep. Back to work. Back to my life. I got new stories to tell.*

REESH. *It has been an honor, GARY THE SMITH. You will always find an open door in Xilna.*
NELLA. *I echo that sentiment, what an absolute pleasure to have made your acquaintance. I speak on behalf of all Flaveyons, we consider you one of our own.*
MOOT. *Still makes no sense what you did and how you did it, but as any Strovian would tell you as one man of the mountain to another...VERY IMPRESSIVE.*
GARY SMITH. *AWWWWW! You guys are the best...getting all emotional like that. And you as well Thart Palls. We're like a CLIMBING FAMILY-you feel that? You pickin' up those ALPINE VIBES between us??? WOW-the SIGNAL IS STRONG-we've got HIGH ALTITUDE HEARTS don't we???!!! I'll see you guys around.*

Gary Smith turns and walks away.
Thart Palls shakes his head.

THART PALLS. *I still cannot figure out how THAT GUY solo climbed the BANASHAK!!!*

Gary Smith stops. Turns. Looks at each of them.

GARY SMITH. *The Banashak? This isn't the Banashak. The Banashak's over there.*

He points, turns, and walks off the peak.

A BANNER drops from the ceiling.
It reads: THE END.
LIGHTS OUT.

Back Matter.

. Kristin Hanggi first read this play in November of 2017. She's been directing it ever since and I'm so grateful.

. Brent French designed the cover of this play-that-is-a-book. We've been friends since 1999. What a gift his friendship is to me.

. Many thanks to Caitlin Elizabeth, who took on this project with joy and a spreadsheet and brought it all together. Caitlin, do not slow your roll.

. To clear things up, the 'E' in Nella's full name-Ornella Vapinius E. Voponomous Montar-stands for 'The Esteemed.' This, of course, raises the obvious question: Why isn't there a 'T.' for the 'The?' Her mother's response: *Because that would make her name too long.*

. A staging note-which is also a question-about the bird on the string on the pole that Chorus 2 moves in circles above the heads of the climbers: What is it made of? Obviously it could be stuffed, like any standard stuffed animal you'd find in a child's bedroom. Fair enough. Perhaps something knitted would add interesting textural and cultural elements, much like a tea cozy or the pair of mittens worn by Bernie Sanders at the 2021 Presidential Inauguration. Rubber is always an option, like the kind used to make a duck. Or a spatula. The playwright requests that paper mache be considered, as it would be lighter and thus easier for Chorus 2 to maneuver.

. Another staging note, this one about the bird as well: CIRCLING BIRD MUSIC sounds exactly as you imagine it.

. Another, other staging note about the bird: The question as to whether the bird is moved in clockwise or counter-clockwise circles is left up to the discretion of Chorus 2 in collaboration with the director. The playwright prefers half and half.

. Many thanks to Kristen Bell, Trace Bell, Ava Lind, Natalie Roy, Jonno Buckley (Jonnotes!), Andrew Morgan, Pete Holmes, Nichole Young and Jeff Tkach who all provided invaluable feedback and laughs.

. Time is bendy.

. A full list of characters:
Mootis Hermanicus Vulner the 12th (Moot)
Thart Palls
Reshafesh Soontamgamonous Milepheshar Steve Sunata
McTavistavish (Reesh)
Ornella Vapinius E. Voponomous Montar (Nella)
Hamoob Aldervin
Reevo
Wilvis Vulner
Helene Weebners
Joonee
Gretchiss
Solonius Maniford
King Shalaj
News Anchor
Lawyer 1
Lawyer 2
Interview Host
Sir Thornan Thornan
Man in small swimsuit who we find out is the king
Swayne Wavers
Stagehand
Reggie Fang
Louis Ortan
Sheila Leela
Donna
Ron Montalban
Linda Meanda
Gary Smith
. A bit about Sheila Leela. She is Reesh's manager, but they used
to be lovers. I know. Everyone is shocked when they hear this.
Sheila and Reesh? Hard to picture, isn't it? But Sheila, you have
to understand, she was there in the beginning. She saw it before
anyone else. What it could be. Who Reesh could be. Sheila was
the one who told him to switch from wearing a silver sash to
wearing a gold sash. And look what *that* did. Moves like that put
Reesh on the map and built the brand. Now here's where things
get a bit dicey: She's now with Louis. *That* Louis. Reesh's
accountant. That's why there was so much added tension in that
meeting. Louis was just trying to do his job but he's also trying to

impress Sheila and Reesh is making it very hard for him to do
that. And Louls, he really wants it to work out with Sheila.
. Within an hour of placing an ad online to sell his car, Gary Smith
received a call from a CALVITH GONIGAN, who had a list of
questions he wanted to ask over the phone before he came to
see the car in person.

GARY SMITH. *All right, fire away.*
CALVITH GONIGAN. *My first question: Is the trunk big enough for
me to transport my bagpipes?*

Gary Smith considered the question.

GARY SMITH. *Well I don't know about that Mr. Gonigan but I
once transported two live penguins, a portable generator and a
small satchel of figs in the trunk for a unit I was doing with my
students called 'Antarctic Escapades.'*

Silence on the other end of the line.
And then Calvith Gonigan quietly responded:

CALVITH GONIGAN. *Whoa. My spirit animal is a penguin.
I'll take the car.*

. I invite you to enjoy this word: *unpigeonholeable.*
. The last unsuccessful attempt to summit The Banashak was by
Nakmon Forgliss, considered by many to be greatest Fargnar-
thian mountaineer ever. Forgliss returned home in shame, only to
begin an entirely new career as a well-respected cheesemonger.
. Someone once told Donna that she's quite *cheugy.* She replied
Thank you. She thought it was a compliment. But then later, in
the parking lot after pilates class, she looked the word up on the
world wide web and she was not happy.
. Remember when Gary Smith was in the pub with his friend
Simon and he was telling Simon about how he could go hiking to
get some new stories and Simon thought that was an excellent
idea so Gary Smith asked Simon if he wanted to come with him
and Simon said he couldn't because he had a dentist appointment and then he had to paint his fence and Gary Smith said he
didn't realize Simon has fence and then Simon said that was why

he had to paint it? Gary Smith thinks about that exchange at least once a day.

. More of my stories and plays-including *We'll Get Back to You* and *Millones Cajones*-are at robbell.com.

photo by marielle chua